Christmas
BEST

www.brightbearbooks.com

ISBN: 978-0-9915233-5-1

Christmas
BEST

**Written
and Illustrated by**

DIANA KIZLAUSKAS

WORKSHOP

BRIGHT BEAR BOOKS

"Do small things
with great love."
— Mother Teresa

To Dalia and Andy —
my Christmas Best

Tap,

Tweak,

Twinkle,

made Christmas toys for girls and boys
in Santa's busy shop.

Tap built houses —
nailed in every tack,

while Tweak made sure the trains ran well

and **never** **left** **the track.**

Dolls, clowns, ponies —
Twinkle gave them smiles,

while Plumperson plumped teddy bears

and Top checked workshop dials.

Then one morning,
Tap began to frown.
"My work is plain and small," he grumped.
He put his hammer down.

"I'm so little
and my job is, too!
That's it, I quit. I'm going to find
IMPORTANT work to do!"

Tweak nudged Twinkle,
"Let's go out and see
if there is bigger Christmas work
for Tap and you and me."

"My job's silly,"
Plumperson complained.
"I push on bumps and pull at lumps.
It leaves me dull and drained."

Top stopped checking.
Thoughts raced through his head.
He spun around and tapped his feet
then raised his arms and said:

"Fine, fresh, flashy —
not like knobs and gears!
Let's venture out and find ourselves
new holiday careers!"

Tap, Tweak, Twinkle,
Plumperson and Top
packed up their things, put on their coats
and left a startled shop.

Bright, bold, bouncy —
they could hardly wait
to do whatever *other* work
would make them grand and **GREAT!**

But every cookie they would make
would burn or smear or break.

Screech, howl, holler —
next, they tried to sing.
The other carolers were shocked.
Their ears began to ring.

Cards, notes, boxes —
they delivered mail.
But Tap got lost and

Tweak's eyes c r o s s e d,

while Top moved like a snail.

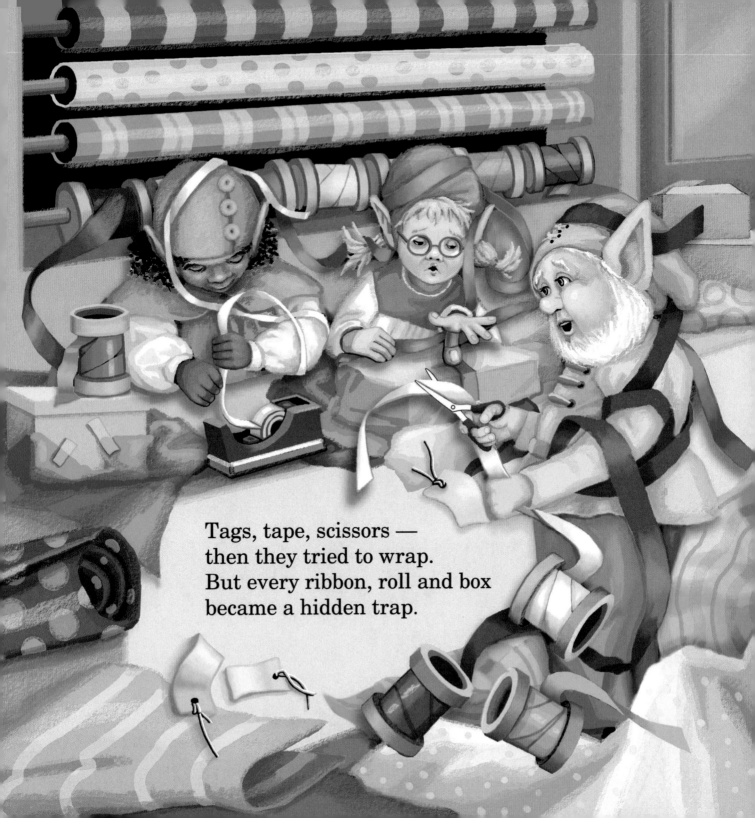

Tags, tape, scissors —
then they tried to wrap.
But every ribbon, roll and box
became a hidden trap.

Spins, leaps, tutus —
dance did not work out.
"Get off the stage, you clumsy elves!"
they heard the people shout.

"What now, windows?
Decorate a store?"
The others rolled their eyes at Tweak.
They shook their heads, "No more!"

"I miss building,"
Tap sat down and sighed.
"I love my dials," Top whispered back,
while Plumperson just cried.

"Where's my sparkle,
where are all my stars?"
poor Twinkle sobbed and Tweak replied,
"I want my railroad cars."

Meanwhile, trouble
swirled around The Pole.
Would boys and girls get stockings filled
with candy canes or *coal*?

Back at Santa's,
things were all AMISS:

S. Claus
1 North Pole

the trains derailed,

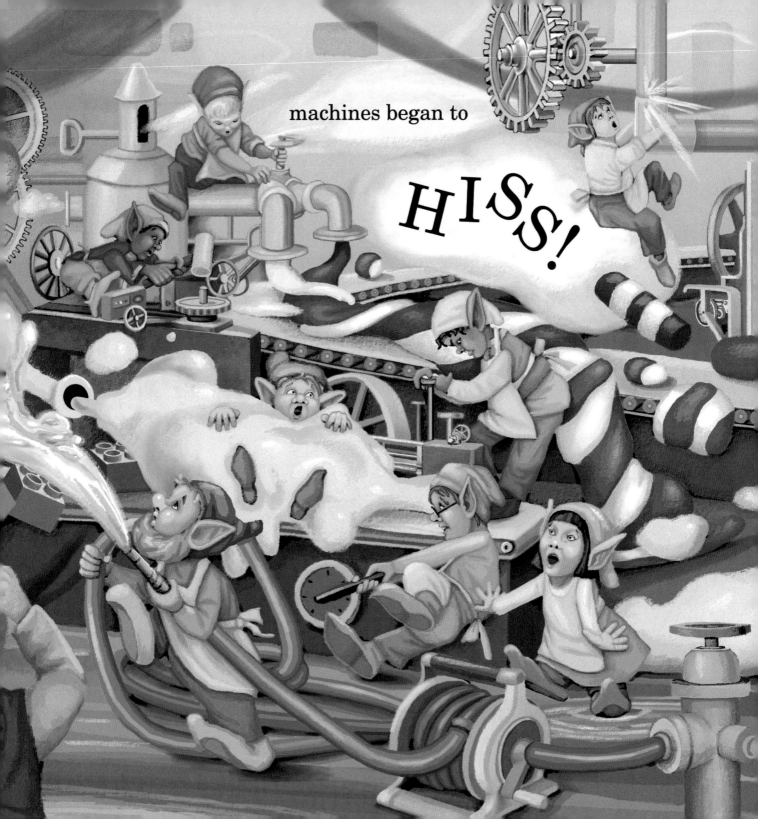

Sad, limp, matted —
teddy bears looked ill,

while dust and cobwebs settled on
Tap's hammer, nails and drill.

"Humpff!" huffed Santa.
"*Not* the time of year
for empty shelves and five good elves
to simply disappear!"

Just then Twinkle
and the other four
snuck back into the workshop
through the cellar door.

Tap, Tweak, Twinkle,
Plumperson and Top
told Santa their adventures were
a wild and wasteful flop.

Wink, smile, chuckle —
Santa hugged each one.
"What makes a job important, friends,
is always **_how_** it's done.

Big, small, tiny —
every task done right,
will fill the world with all your love
and make the Season bright!

We're all special,
great in our own way!
The best we have to give will make

a DAZZLING

holiday!"

Then he shouted,
"Go and join the rest!
Go nail and paint and plump and check
and do your **CHRISTMAS BEST**!"

Tap, Tweak, Twinkle,
Plumperson and Top
went back to do what they did best
in Santa's busy shop.

So each present
got to Santa's sleigh
and reached the home of every child
in time for Christmas Day.

Santa's helpers
learned what Santa knew:
their best would always make them great
and bless the whole world, too!

DIANA KIZLAUSKAS

is a Chicago area artist whose children's illustrations have been published by nationally and internationally known companies including Harcourt Achieve; Macmillan McGraw-Hill; Pearson Education/Scott Foresman; Compass/Seed Media; Pauline Books and Media; EDCO/Ireland and others. Most recently, she has both written and illustrated LETTUCE! and Christmas Best, published independently under the imprint of Bright Bear Books.

She is a member of The Society of Children's Book Writers and Illustrators.

Visit Diana at her website:

www. dianakizlauskas.com

Made in the USA
Middletown, DE
06 December 2022

17262214R00031